Contents

FOLK TALES FROM ASIA
FOR CHILDREN EVERYWHERE

Book Four

sponsored by the
Asian Cultural Centre for Unesco

New York · WEATHERHILL/HEIBONSHA · Tokyo

This is the fourth volume of Asian folk tales to be published under the Asian Copublication Programme carried out, in cooperation with Unesco, by the Asian Cultural Centre for Unesco / Tokyo Book Development Centre. The stories have been selected and, with the editorial help of the publishers, edited by a five-country central editorial board in consultation with the Unesco member states in Asia.

First edition, 1976
Second printing, 1982

Jointly published by John Weatherhill, Inc., 149 Madison Avenue, New York, New York 10016, with editorial offices at 7-6-13 Roppongi, Minato-ku, Tokyo; and Heibonsha, Tokyo. Copyright © 1976 by the Asian Cultural Centre for Unesco / Tokyo Book Development Centre, 6 Fukuro-machi, Shinjuku-ku, Tokyo. Printed in Japan.

LIBRARY OF CONGRESS CATALOGING IN PUBLICATION DATA: Main entry under title: Folk tales from Asia for children everywhere / Book 3-: lacks series statement / "Sponsored by the Asian Cultural Centre for Unesco" / SUMMARY: A multi-volume collection of traditional folk tales from various Asian countries illustrated by native artists / 1. Tales, Asian / [1. Folklore—Asian] / I. Yunesuko Ajia Bunka Sentā / PZ8.1F717 / 398.2'095 [E] / 74-82605 / ISBN 0-8348-1035-2

The Crocodile and the Jackal

Once upon a time there was a jackal who lived in a forest. He was very clever and very tricky. A river flowed through the same forest, and in it lived a crocodile.

The crocodile had seven sons, and he wanted them to get a good education. When they began growing up he started looking for a teacher for them. Remembering that the jackal was well known as a scholar, one afternoon he went to the river bank and waited for the jackal to pass by.

Just at sundown the jackal came to the river. He was frightened when he saw the crocodile waiting for him. But the crocodile reassured him and said: "I have something important to discuss with you. Please

H. Khan

come closer and let's talk." So the jackal came and sat beside the crocodile.

The crocodile asked the jackal to become the teacher of his seven sons. The idea pleased the jackal, but instead of showing his pleasure he said: "I'm very busy in the afternoons catching crabs. And during the mornings I teach my own children. But if you could bring your sons to my place every day, I could give them lessons at the same time."

"That would be fine," said the crocodile, "but they're still very young and it would be too far for them to make the trip to your home and back every day. Instead, couldn't they stay at your place during the week?"

This was just what the jackal wanted and he quickly agreed. So the next morning the crocodile brought his seven sons to the jackal's den. The jackal's mouth began to water when he saw the seven plump crocodile children. But he hid his greed and began to make a great show of petting the boys. Then, turning to the father, he said: "Well, brother, you can go now. I'll take the kids into my den and give them their first lesson."

After the father had gone, the jackal started prodding the plump children with his fingers, smacking his lips and thinking how sweet they would taste. Then he got out his spelling book and started the first lesson. Prodding each crocodile child in turn, he said:

"E-A-T spells 'eat,'
M-E-A-T spells 'meat'—
How do you like that,
My crocodile sweet?"

The children, of course, didn't even know the alphabet, so how could they say whether they liked "eat" and "meat"? They sat silent for some time and then began running around playing. The jackal pretended to be dozing, but he kept watching them from under his eyelids. Thinking he was asleep, the children gradually began slipping outside, one by one, to play. When only one of them was left with the jackal, he suddenly opened his eyes and grabbed the crocodile child.

"Where do you think you're running off to?" the jackal said. And before the crocodile child could answer, the jackal gobbled him up, head and tail and all.

Next day the crocodile father came to see his children. He waited

6

outside the den and asked the jackal to call them. The jackal picked up the six remaining children one by one and showed them to the crocodile. Then he picked up the sixth child a second time and showed him to the father, who went home happy and contented.

At the next lesson, the jackal again said to each child:

> "E-A-T spells 'eat,'
> M-E-A-T spells 'meat'—
> How do you like that,
> My crocodile sweet?"

And then he promptly gobbled up another crocodile child, head and tail and all.

When the crocodile father came the next morning to see his sons, the jackal picked up the five remaining children one by one and showed them to the father. Then he picked up the fifth child twice more and showed him to the father, who went home happy and contented.

And it went on like this day after day until the jackal had gobbled up all seven crocodile children, heads and tails and all. Then he ran away from his den and went to live far away.

When the father came to the den the next day and called for his children, no one answered. The den was empty. Finally he realized what had happened and he determined to take his revenge on the jackal. He began looking for him everywhere. But he couldn't find him.

After a long time the jackal began to be homesick for his old den. Thinking that the crocodile had forgotten about his eating the children, he returned to his den. But the crocodile had not forgotten. Secretly he followed the jackal wherever he went, waiting for a chance to take his revenge.

At last one day the chance came. The crocodile hid himself in a small canal under a clump of water hyacinths. The jackal waded into the canal to catch some frogs for a meal. Suddenly the crocodile lunged forward and caught one of the jackal's legs in his strong teeth. He said: "And where do you think you'll run off to now, Mr. Jackal, my fine scholar?"

But the jackal was still full of tricks. He said: "Well, well. First let go of my walking stick, and I'll explain everything to you."

Hearing this, the crocodile thought he had in fact caught the jackal's walking stick instead of his leg. So he let go to catch a real leg. With a leap, the jackal was off, running for his life, and after that he was very careful not to get near the crocodile.

But the crocodile did not give up so easily and kept waiting his chance. One day he saw a bush full of ripe blackberries hanging over the river. Knowing how much the jackal liked blackberries, he hid himself under the bush and waited. Presently the jackal came along. First he saw the blackberries and then he saw the crocodile's tracks on the river bank. He thought the crocodile might be hiding there. To make sure he called out: "Hey, you blackberry bush, why are you so still? Why don't you sway in the wind?"

Hearing these words, the crocodile began shaking the bush. Then the jackal said: "Oh, you stupid crocodile! It's you hiding under that bush."

The crocodile made a furious dash and tried to catch the jackal, but once again the jackal went running away into the forest. So the crocodile had to continue waiting his chance.

There came a time when food became very scarce in the forest, and the jackal was very hungry. Unable to find anything to eat in the forest, he made up his mind to catch crabs from the river despite the crocodile. Stealing to the river, he put his tail down a crab hole and waited quietly for a crab to catch hold so he could pull it out.

Now, the crocodile had been searching everywhere for his enemy. He was searching again today and suddenly he smelled the jackal from

9

a distance. Sniffing, he followed the jackal smell to the crab hole. The jackal was dreaming about the juicy crab he was going to catch and didn't hear the crocodile coming.

Suddenly the crocodile lunged forward and clamped his strong teeth around the jackal's tail.

Immediately the jackal cried out: "Hey, brother crocodile, please let go of my fishing net, and I'll explain everything to you."

Fishing net or not, the crocodile did not let go this time. Tugging and jerking, he pulled the jackal down into the river.

And that was one jackal who never played tricks again.

Retold by Halima Khatun
Translated by Kabir Chowdhury
Illustrated by Hashem Khan

10

The Old Woman and the Hare

Once there was a very cunning hare. He loved adventures. Sometimes he acted as a judge, showing such wisdom and such a sense of justice that everyone called him Judge Hare. But at other times he was full of mischief and enjoyed playing tricks on people, sometimes to get out of a difficult situation and sometimes just for the fun of it.

Now, there was an old woman who often went to the village market to buy bananas, which she would take home and sell to her neighbors at a small profit. Her path led through a clearing in the forest where Judge Hare lived. Whenever he saw her coming back from the market with a basket of bananas on her head, he longed to eat some of them. So he started thinking how to trick the old woman.

"Maybe," he told himself, "if I made a frightening noise, the old

woman would think it was a ghost and drop the bananas and run for her life . . . But I don't have a big enough mouth to make a big enough noise . . . Maybe, then, I should ask the tiger to help me by roaring . . . But then he'd want a share of the bananas, and I certainly don't want to give even one away."

He thought and thought, and at last he had a good idea. "Humans are very fond of hare stew," he told himself, "but they can't catch a hare very often. How often have I seen them hunting hares all day

long without being able to catch a single one. So if I lie down in the old woman's path and pretend to be dead, she'll be delighted to find me."

Sure enough, the next day when the old woman found a fat hare lying in the path, she gave a cry of delight. She bent over the hare to look closely. "Is he really dead, I wonder, or only wounded?" she asked herself. "No, he looks quite dead, but he's still warm, so he must have just died. What a delicious stew he'll make!"

She put her basket on the ground and, picking up the hare, laid him on top of the bananas. Then she put the basket back on her head and went on her way toward home.

"I mustn't forget to get some lemons for the stew," she told herself. "And he's such a big hare that I can save half to eat tomorrow."

While the poor old woman was happily thinking about the delicious stew she was going to make, the hare, up in the basket, was happily peeling and eating the bananas one by one.

When the old woman reached home she lowered the basket from her

head. At that instant the hare jumped out and went running away. Before the bewildered old woman realized what was happening, the hare had escaped.

Looking in the basket, the old woman found it contained only empty banana peels. "That was surely Judge Hare in my basket!" she cried aloud. "Only he could have cheated me so cleverly. He may be a good, wise judge, but when he starts playing tricks, he's a very bad hare. Doesn't he know that just one wicked trick turns a good person into a bad one?"

But Judge Hare was much too far away to hear the old woman's cries. He had disappeared into the forest and was already planning his next adventure.

Retold by Ken Khun
Translated by Thach Tan Khoang
Illustrated by Huot Thun

The White Elephant

Shankar was the rajah's chief gardener. He worked from dawn to dusk in the royal gardens that stretched for miles—multicolored flower beds, lush green lawns, and clumps of majestic trees. He swept the leaves, watered the flowers, tended the young plants and saplings, rooted out weeds, raked and manured the soil, and trimmed the hedges. From his cottage in a corner of the garden, where he lived with his wife Lakshmi, he kept an eye on things.

One night Shankar couldn't sleep. He tossed and turned till midnight. Then he sat up and casually looked out the window. He couldn't believe his eyes! Surely his eyes were deceiving him! He looked again. In the silvery moonlight a huge white elephant was quietly plucking and nibbling at the fresh green grass.

Shankar was completely perplexed. Where could the elephant have come from? Besides, it was white, and Shankar had never seen a white elephant before. Suddenly a thought struck him. He remembered that, when he was a boy, his mother had often told him stories of the gods who dwelt in heaven. Indra was their king and he rode Airavata, a beautiful elephant whose skin was as white as snow.

"Surely this is Airavata!" Shankar exclaimed excitedly. "Tired of the delicacies in heaven, he must have flown down to earth for a change. If I can hold onto his tail, he will take me back with him and I shall see all the wonders of heaven."

Shankar jumped out of bed, tiptoed out of the house so as not to wake his wife, and ran quietly toward the elephant.

Hiding behind a tree, Shankar watched the elephant. After eating the grass, the elephant turned toward the tender leaves of the saplings and the half-ripened fruit on the mango trees. Shankar didn't utter even a murmur of protest. He was so anxious to go to heaven that he didn't want to risk offending the elephant.

Just as dawn was breaking, the elephant finished his meal. He raised his trunk and trumpeted with satisfaction. Shankar knew it was time for him to leave. He ran up and caught hold of the elephant's tail. Airavata rose like a bird. Soon he was flying high above the clouds. Shankar looked down cautiously. The royal gardens were just a speck in the distance.

They landed in heaven. Shankar released Airavata's tail and looked around him. His eyes filled with wonder. "This must be paradise—the garden of heaven!" he exclaimed delightedly. "Look how big and beautiful the trees are! I wonder what kind of manure Indra's gardener uses." Shankar wandered around marveling at everything. The trees were ten times larger than those on earth, the leaves ten times as lush, the fruit ten times as tasty, and the flowers ten times as colorful. Shankar spent the day touching the leaves, feasting his eyes on the flowers, and tasting the juicy, delicious fruit around him.

At dusk, he suddenly remembered his wife waiting for him at home. He knew how worried she would be about him. "I'll take her something—a present from heaven," he decided.

He chose an areca nut that was as large as a coconut, and a betel leaf as big as a banana leaf. He and his wife loved chewing them. As soon as night fell, the elephant trumpeted. It was time to return to earth. Shankar ran and grasped his tail. In a few minutes he was back in the royal gardens. He rushed home to his wife, who had been waiting anxiously for him.

"Where have you been all this time?" she asked angrily.

"Don't be angry," replied Shankar. "See what I've brought for you." And he showed her the areca nut and betel leaf.

Lakshmi was amazed. "Where did you get such giant-sized things?" she asked excitedly.

"From heaven, of course," Shankar replied and told her the whole story. At first she wouldn't believe him, but right before her eyes were the enormous areca nut and betel leaf. She was convinced at last. Then Shankar warned: "You must keep this a secret. This marvelous areca

18

and betel will keep us chewing at least a week. But be careful not to let anyone else into our secret."

Lakshmi readily promised, but she found it very difficult to keep her word. She liked to talk. When Shankar made another trip to heaven and returned with an enormous mango that was the most delicious she had ever tasted in her life, she became even more eager to tell her friends of her luck. But she resisted the temptation.

Then her husband went to heaven a third time and brought back a gigantic flower whose fragrance filled the whole cottage.

One of her friends said: "What wonderful perfume you're using! Where did you get it?"

"I'm not using any perfume," replied Lakshmi. "That's the fragrance of my giant flower."

One thing led to another, and soon Lakshmi was telling her friend the whole story. Of course, she made her promise not to tell anyone else.

The friend promised but, being a gossip, could not keep the secret. So she told it to her friend, after making *her* promise not to tell it to anyone else. Her closest friend readily promised, but she too told it to *her* friend, who promised not to tell anyone else. And so it continued, till soon all the women of the town knew the secret. And they told their husbands. Before long the whole town knew Shankar's secret.

One morning, all the people of the town came flocking to Shankar's cottage. They insisted on going with Shankar on his next trip to heaven.

Shankar was furious at his wife's folly. But what could he do? So he reluctantly agreed: "Come to the royal gardens tonight."

That night the royal gardens presented a strange sight. There were more men and women than there were trees, but while the trees swayed with the wind, the human beings were as still as if they had been carved in marble. Even when Airavata appeared, no one stirred or uttered a sound.

20

At dawn, Shankar beckoned silently. Then he rushed up and grasped the elephant's tail. Lakshmi held onto her husband's feet. Her friend held Lakshmi's feet, the friend's husband held his wife's feet, another man held his feet, and that man's wife held her husband's

feet, and so on. When the white elephant rose into the air, a long chain of men and women trailed after him on his journey to heaven, each one clinging to the one above him.

During the trip, the last woman in the chain couldn't contain her curiosity. "Lakshmi told us that the fruit and flowers from heaven are very, very big," she said to her husband. "But she didn't say exactly how big. Please ask your friend above to find out."

So her husband asked the man above him. The man asked his wife, who asked the woman above her. The woman asked her husband, who asked the man above him, and so on. Ultimately, Lakshmi was asked the question, and she said to her husband: "They want to know exactly how big the fruit and flowers in heaven are."

"You'll see for yourself when we reach heaven," replied Shankar curtly, and his answer was passed down the chain.

But the woman at the end of the chain was so impatient that she kept repeating her question. At last Lakshmi implored her husband: "She refuses to wait. You must tell her immediately how large the fruit and flowers in heaven are."

Shankar was so upset at this foolish impatience that he said angrily: "Each fruit is ten times as big as a fruit on earth. You know that the areca nut was this big. . ." To demonstrate the size with his hands, Shankar released the elephant's tail and . . .

The entire chain all the way from Shankar, whose feet were held by Lakshmi, whose feet were held by her friend, whose feet were held by her husband, whose feet were held by his friend, down to that last impatient woman, came tumbling down to earth.

Retold by Leelawati Bhagwat
Illustrated by Pranab Chakravarty

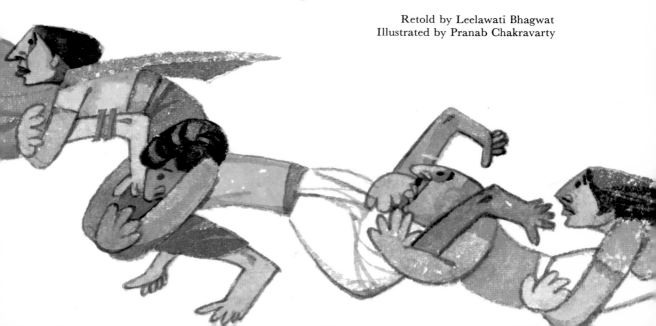

The Old Man with a Wen

A long, long time ago, in a distant mountain village, there was a kind old man who had a huge wen on the side of his chin. The wen was as big as his fist and flopped from side to side whenever he moved. More than anything in the world the old man wanted to get rid of his wen. It got in the way when he tried to eat, and everyone in the village poked fun at him. But how could he get rid of the awful thing?

One day, as usual, he went deep into the mountain forest to gather firewood. He stacked the wood on his A-frame, put the load on his back, and started down the mountain. The sun was sinking fast and he hurried to reach home before darkness fell. But the path was dim and the heavy load made him tired. His breath came in short gasps and sweat started running down his face. Unable to go farther, he took the A-frame off and propped it up beside the path while he sat down to rest.

"It's getting so dark that I can't possibly find my way home," he muttered to himself. "Where can I spend the night?"

Just then he saw in the distance the dim outline of an old tumble-down hut with a thatched roof. "Good!" he told himself. "I'll just go and ask if I can stay there for the night." And he hurried toward the house.

"Hello!" he shouted. "Anybody home?" But there was no answer. The house seemed deserted.

He went into the house and lay down on the floor. But the deserted house frightened him and he couldn't sleep. He started to sing so that he would forget he was afraid. The sound of his voice carried far into the deep, dark, quiet forest. The more he sang the braver he felt.

Suddenly he heard a voice from somewhere saying: "Here it is. Here!" He wondered who could be out there in the middle of the night. He stopped singing and sat up straight.

The door opened and in strode a tokkebi, a huge, horrible-looking kind of goblin with a horn growing from his head. Behind him came a line of tokkebis, all dancing and laughing loudly.

24

The old man was so frightened that he started to tremble. But he told himself that he mustn't show fear before the tokkebis. So he managed somehow to look calm and unafraid, and then he went right on singing as if nothing strange had happened. The tokkebis put their hands behind their ears and listened intently to his singing. After a while they started to dance.

All night the old man sang and sang, and all night the tokkebis danced and danced. He knew he would be saved if he could keep them dancing until morning, because tokkebis must return home when the sun rises. Finally, just as dawn was about to break, the leader of the tokkebis came up to the old man and said: "We've never heard such beautiful singing before. What is your secret? Where does such a beautiful sound come from?"

"From my throat, of course," said the old man. "Where else?"

The tokkebis stared at the huge flopping wen on the old man's chin and said: "No, the sound seems to be coming from that big bag under your chin. We love the sound of your singing. Won't you sell it to us? We'll pay you well for your singing bag."

Surprised, the old man asked: "How can you take the bag off my chin?"

The tokkebis laughed heartily and their leader said: "Don't you worry about that. If you'll sell it, we'll get it off without hurting you."

"Well," said the old man, "you're welcome to it."

He really didn't want to cheat the tokkebis and would have been happy to give them his wen. But they brought a large bag full of gold and precious stones and dumped the contents on the floor in front of him. While he sat staring at the treasure, he suddenly realized that the tokkebi leader had the wen in his hands. He hadn't even felt anything when they removed it from his chin.

The sun rose and the tokkebis vanished. He rubbed the place where the wen had been: it was as smooth as smooth can be. Joyfully, he put the gold and jewels on top of his load of wood, put the A-frame on his back, and returned to the village.

Everyone was astonished to see the old man without the wen on his chin. They were also very envious of his becoming rich so suddenly.

Soon word spread to the next village. In that village there was another old man with a wen on the side of his chin. Hearing the story, he became very greedy, wanting some treasure for himself. So he went to visit the first old man, who told him everything that had happened.

After hearing the story, the second old man decided to do the same. That very day he went into the mountains to the deserted house. It was still daylight, so he lay down to have a nap without even bothering to gather firewood. When he awoke, night had come. He went inside the old house and started to sing. Soon the tokkebis began to gather. The greedy old man sang louder and louder. The tokkebis, bending over with laughter, entered the room and the old man welcomed them gladly.

The leader came forward and said: "You sing well. Where does the beautiful sound come from?"

The greedy old man, who wanted treasure even more than he wanted to get rid of his wen, quickly answered: "The sound comes from this

bag on the side of my neck. If you'd like to buy it, I'd be willing to sell it to you for some treasure."

"What do you take us for!" screamed the tokkebis with loud voices. "Several days ago we bought one of those bags and it didn't work at all. We won't be tricked again!"

With these words they brought out the wen they had taken from the kind old man and stuck it on the other side of the greedy old man's chin. "This will help you sing even better," they said, and then they disappeared.

So now, instead of having sold his wen for gold and precious stones, the greedy old man had two of them, one on either side of his chin. He sat there, empty-handed, and sobbed and sobbed.

Retold by Hyo-seon O
Translated by Genell Y. Poitras
Illustrated by Yong-ju Kim

29

Aren't We All Human Beings?

Once a king was taking a long trip in his royal barge accompanied by another boat for the royal advisors. It was a hot, sunny day, and the boatmen had to row upstream for many hours, while the king and his advisors lay at ease under the canopies of the boats.

The boatmen's bodies were covered with sweat, and one of them began grumbling. "It's really not fair," he said to the boatman next to him. "Aren't we all human beings? Why do *we* have to do all the

hard work while those lazy advisors just rest in the shade? After all,
we're all men and all subjects of the king, so they ought to be rowing
too."

The king's eyes were closed, but he heard everything the boatman
said. However, he pretended to go on sleeping.

At the end of the day they tied up beside a small temple to sleep in
their boats. After they had eaten, the boatmen fell asleep quickly; some
of them were even snoring. But the king was still awake and he heard
a noise coming from the direction of the temple. He awakened the
boatman who had been grumbling and sent him to see what the noise
was.

31

When the boatman returned, the king said: "What is the noise?"

"Some puppies are making the noise," answered the boatman.

"How many puppies are there?" asked the king.

The boatman didn't know, so he had to run back to check. When he returned, he said: "There're five puppies."

"Are the puppies male or female?" asked the king.

Again the boatman had to run to see. Returning, he told the king: "There are three male puppies and two female puppies."

"What color are they?" asked the king.

Again the boatman ran to see. When he came back, he said: "They are white, black, and brown."

Then the king wakened one of the royal advisors and asked him to go and see what the noise was.

In a few minutes the advisor came back and said: "It's some puppies that are making the noise."

"How many puppies?" asked the king.

"Five," answered the advisor.

"Are they males or females?" asked the king.

"Three males and two females."

"What color are they?"

"The puppies are white, black, and brown, and the mother is black. They belong to the priest of the temple there."

Then the king turned to the boatman and said: "You had to go four times to answer my questions, but my advisor had to go only once. That's why some men are boatmen and some are royal advisors, even though we're all human beings."

Retold by Thit Boon Phoydouangdi
Translated by Sang Seunsom
Illustrated by K. Luangraj

33

The Fanged Raja

Once there was a country called Kedah. The ruler of the country had such large eyeteeth that he was called the Fanged Raja. He was still young and did not know how to rule. He did whatever he pleased and would never listen to the advice of the four ministers who were the royal advisors.

The people of Kedah all hated their raja. Not a day passed without someone's being arrested for disrespect to the raja. Without even finding out whether they had actually done anything bad or not, the raja would have them tortured and thrown into prison.

Now, the raja was extremely fond of spinach. It was his favorite food and he ate it every day. One day to his surprise he found that his spinach tasted better than ever before. So he called his chief cook, a woman named Gerau, and asked her what she had put in the spinach. Even when he was pleased, as now, he always spoke so harshly that people thought he was angry.

At first Gerau was too frightened to answer. The raja pulled out his dagger and threatened to kill her unless she told him.

Finally the woman said: "Please forgive me, O Great Raja, but while preparing the spinach today I accidentally cut one of my fingers."

"What happened then?" the raja interrupted impatiently.

"The blood from the cut dropped into the spinach," she said. "And I was in such a hurry that I didn't have time to wash the spinach again."

"So that's the reason it tasted so good," the raja said, smiling and nodding as he dismissed the cook.

The next day the raja was in the audience hall. All his ministers, including the four royal advisors, were present, as well as his warriors and many chiefs. The raja called his chief attendant and said: "As of today, one of the prisoners is to be killed each day."

The chief attendant, who was bowing low before the royal dais, trembled with fear and said: "May I ask the purpose, O Mighty One?"

"Don't ask questions," said the raja. "Just kill a prisoner each day and give his blood to Gerau, the chief cook. She'll know what to do. Now go."

The chief attendant was about to go, reluctantly, to carry out the royal command when he was stopped by the royal advisors. "Now wait a minute," they said. "Don't be too quick about killing people who may not be guilty at all."

"But it's a royal command," said the chief attendant.

"We know," said the advisors, "but you mustn't hurry to do something that's not right."

"Your Majesty," the chief attendant said to the raja, "the royal advisors say I should not kill the prisoners."

The raja became very angry. "What I do is my business!" he cried, his face red as fire.

"But you're being unjust and cruel," protested the advisors. "No king in the world would do what you're about to do."

"This is my business!" thundered the raja.

"But, Your Majesty, you just can't do whatever you like."

"Silence!" cried the raja. Then he turned to the chief attendant and said sternly: "Go at once and do as I command."

The chief attendant was so frightened that he dared not argue any further. As for Gerau, she was even more frightened and dared not protest at all. So each day she prepared the raja's spinach mixed with the blood of one of the prisoners.

From that day onward the raja became crueler and crueler. He did whatever he pleased. The people became angrier and angrier, but they were afraid to rise against the raja. The four royal advisors fled from the palace, and the entire kingdom was filled with fear and hatred.

Word of the Fanged Raja's cruelty finally reached the ears of Kampar the Fighter, who lived in the mountains. Now, Kampar had the magical power of turning himself into almost anything, and he decided to teach the raja a lesson. Leaving the mountains, he came down to the

city. Then he began telling everyone he met how cruel and wicked the raja was. Wherever he went in the city he was always speaking out loudly against the raja. And very soon he got what he wanted: he was arrested and brought before the raja.

"So you're the man who dares speak against me!" said the raja. "Just who do you think you are to go around saying such bad things about me, your raja?"

"I'm a man who knows right from wrong," said Kampar defiantly. "You're a wicked man and don't deserve to be a raja. I'll keep right on saying so in the loudest voice I have."

These words made the raja furious. He whipped out his sword and was about to cut Kampar down. But then he said: "No, I won't even touch such dirt as you." Handing his sword to one of his warriors, he commanded: "Take this sword and kill him. Don't let him live another moment. Kill him! Kill him!"

"Now, now," said Kampar, "it's unjust, you know, to kill a man without first having an investigation and calling witnesses."

The raja became still angrier at these disrespectful words. "How dare you speak like that to me!" he bellowed. Taking back his sword, he said: "All right, then, I'll have the pleasure of cutting off your head with my own hands. Take your last breath, because you will never be able to tell lies about your raja again."

Kampar laughed tauntingly. "Your Majesty," he said, "surely you wouldn't kill a man while his hands were tied; surely even such a wicked raja as you couldn't be that much of a coward."

"All right," said the raja, "I'll free you and then cut your head off." With these words he cut the rope from Kampar's hands.

"Thank you, Your Majesty," said Kampar, laughing loudly. "Now you just try drinking my blood!"

The raja was so enraged he could no longer control himself. His face was red as blood and his lips quivered. He swung his sword at Kampar's head, but Kampar dodged. Again and again the raja cut at Kampar, but the man remained unhurt.

The raja then ordered all his warriors to kill Kampar and they prepared to attack. Just at the moment when they were about to cut him down, Kampar closed his eyes and made a silent wish.

Lo and behold! in a flash Kampar the Fighter had turned into a huge tiger.

"Kill the tiger!" shouted the raja. But the warriors were so frightened they didn't dare move.

"Kill the tiger!" the raja roared again.

The tiger roared even more loudly than the raja, and the warriors were now so frightened that they were trembling all over. Suddenly they whirled around and ran for their lives out of the palace.

"Don't run!" called the raja. "Come back and fight!"

But no warrior was left to heed the raja, who now became frightened too. The tiger was moving slowly toward him.

"Help!" cried the raja. And he too took to his heels, running out of the palace.

The tiger went running after the raja. The royal advisors, hearing the commotion, came running up and they too joined in the chase after the cruel raja. The raja ran and ran, with the tiger hot on his heels. He ran right through the city and deep into the jungle. And he never came back.

Retold by Zubaidah Abdul Rahman
Translated by Dahlan A. Wahab
Illustrated by Mohamed Ali

41

The Doko

Once upon a time in a certain village there was a poor family of four —a man and his wife, their young son, and the man's old father. The old man had worked hard for many, many years, and now he was too old to work any more. So he was entirely dependent upon his son and daughter-in-law for his living, and they found him a great burden.

As time went on the old man became more and more of a bother to them. He needed much help, but neither his son nor his daughter-in-law wanted to take care of him. He had to eat whatever scraps they gave him and wear whatever thin, old clothes came his way. He was

often cold and hungry. Sometimes the boy would feel so sorry for his old grandfather that he'd share his own food with him, but his parents would scold him if they saw what he was doing, telling him he mustn't waste good food.

The old man was unhappy about the way he was treated, and he was always grumbling and complaining. But instead of trying to comfort him, the man and his wife would just repeat an old proverb to each other: "An old ox stumbles and an old man complains."

Things went from bad to worse. The old man grew more and more fussy, and his son and daughter-in-law grew more and more impatient. Finally, they simply couldn't stand the old man any longer. Secretly they began planning how to get rid of him. They decided to take the old man to some place far, far away and leave him there. The man said that he would go to the market and buy a doko, a large basket of coarsely woven bamboo, to carry his old father away in.

"I'll take him to some place so far away that he can't possibly make his way back and I'll leave him under a tree by the roadside. Then maybe people will feel sorry for him and take care of him," said the man.

"But what about our neighbors?" asked the wife. "They'll soon notice that Father is no longer here. What'll we say when they ask about him?"

"Just say that he wanted to be taken to some holy place where he could spend the rest of his life in peace," the husband answered.

Thus they made their plans. But without their realizing it, their son had overheard their conversation. As soon as his father had left for the market to get the doko, the boy asked: "Mother, why are you going to throw Grandfather away?"

"No, no!" his mother answered hurriedly. "We're not going to throw him away. Of course we aren't. You see, there's no one here to take good care of him, since both your father and I must work hard. So your father has decided to take Grandfather to a place where he'll get more attention."

"Where is the place?" asked the boy.

"Oh, it's far away. It's a place you don't even know."

"And who will look after Grandfather there?"

"Don't you worry about that. There'll be many kind people there to look after him," the mother said reassuringly.

Toward sundown the man came back with a large doko. He waited until it was night, for he didn't want the neighbors to see what he was doing. When it was quite dark, he lifted the old man into the doko.

"What's this all about?" asked the old man, alarmed. "Where are you going to take me in this doko?"

"Father, you know that my wife and I can't take care of you much longer. So we decided to take you to a holy place where everyone will be kind to you," the man replied. "You'll be far better off there."

But the old man wasn't deceived. He immediately understood what they intended to do with him. "You ungrateful son!" he shouted. "Just think of all those years I took care of you while you were growing up—and this is how you pay me back!" And he began to shout curses at his son and daughter-in-law.

The man became angry. With a jerk he lifted the doko onto his back and hurried out of the house.

The boy had been watching all this in silence. Just when his father was about to disappear into the night, the boy called out to him: "Father, even if you have to throw Grandfather away, please take good care of the doko and bring it back."

44

Puzzled by the boy's words, the man stopped, turned back, and asked: "Why, my son?"

"Because," came the boy's innocent answer, "we'll be needing it again when you're old and I have to throw you away."

At the boy's words, the man's legs began to wobble. Somehow he couldn't take another step forward. So he turned around and brought his old father home again.

Retold by Shyam Das Baishnab
Translated by Abhi Subedi
Illustrated by Tek Bir Mukhiya

The Tale of Tao

Time was when the sky hung very close above the earth, so close indeed that you could reach up and touch it without even standing on your toes. That was also the time when there was only one human being in all the world. This was a man whose name was Tao.

Being all alone, Tao had no human companions, but he did have two very good friends—Lang-it or Sky, and Lup-a or Earth. They were very dear to him, and he to them, and the three often talked together of many things, both great and small.

Tao lived in a little hut made of dried palm leaves. Besides his two friends, he had a few treasures. There were the two big round lamps that he kept on opposite sides of his hut. One was called Buwan or Moon; it was the color of silver and shimmered with a soft silvery light. The other was Araw or Sun; it was yellow and glowed like golden grains of rice.

There was also Bituin, Tao's belt of a thousand stars. He wore Star Belt at night to keep him from wandering in his sleep, and when morning came he would hang it on the central post of his hut as he went about his work. Then there was his guitar. He played it every night before he went to sleep and again in the morning when he woke up. And he also had a big mortar and pestle, which he used for pounding the precious rice that was his food.

Tao would tie the silver lamp, Moon, in Sky's hair before going to sleep. Each time he would say: "Ay, Sky, how beautiful you look with Moon glowing in your hair!"

But Sky was very modest and would answer: "Yes, Tao, but see how Earth also shines in the soft light of Moon."

Earth would say: "Yes, Tao, but see how Moon's beauty shines on your face. Moonlight and shadows come through the leaves and paint patterns on your brown face."

Then the three would sing together at nightfall, while Tao strummed his guitar. Since it was night, they would sing to the silver lamp, Moon, as it hung in the sky:

47

48

"O Moon, how lovely you are! Ay!
Spread your soft arms about us
And charm us to sleep. Ay! Ay!"

Finally, drowsy with sleep, Tao would fasten Star Belt around him and go to bed.

At dawn Tao would return Star Belt to the post. Then he would go out and take Moon from Sky's hair, keeping it in his hut during the day. In its place he would tie the golden lamp, Sun, in Sky's hair and say: "Ay, Earth, how fresh and warm Sun makes you as it hangs in Sky's hair."

Earth would answer modestly: "Yes, Tao, but see how Sky also glows in Sun's strong rays."

Sky would say: "Yes, Tao, but see how Sun's strength shows on your face. Shadow and light fall on the rippling water yonder and paint patterns on your brown face."

Then the three would sing together at daybreak, while Tao strummed his guitar. Since it was day, they would sing to the golden lamp, Sun:

"O Sun, how strong you are! Ay!
Spread your powerful arms about us
And help us in our work. Ay! Ay!"

Then Tao would go about the day's work. When the rains fell, he sowed and planted rice in his terraced fields. In the dry season he harvested the rice. Then he would thresh the rice to remove the grain from the golden husks, after which he would pound the rice with his mortar and pestle.

In this way Tao lived peacefully and happily with his two good friends and his treasures. But Tao and Sky and Earth were such very good friends that they often could not keep from meddling in each other's business. And thus, one bright day, they had a terrible quarrel.

Tao was pounding rice and became very tired. His arms kept going up and down, up and down. "Thud! thud! thud!" went the pestle as Tao's strong hands kept beating it in the mortar.

"Ay! ay!" sighed Tao. "I'm really getting tired of this hard work."

"What are you complaining about?" asked Earth. "It's work you must do, isn't it?"

49

"Yes, indeed," Sky chimed in. "After all, that's the only work you have to do. Don't the gods protect your crop so you can have a good harvest and plenty of golden rice?"

Earth added: "And don't the gods make me yield fruits for you to pick? Fish to catch? Water to drink? And, above all, nourishment to make your rice grains large and plentiful?"

"Thud! thud! thud!" went the pestle as Tao pounded harder and harder.

"Ay! ay! ay!" went Tao, still complaining.

Soon Sky quite lost patience. He screamed: "Stop your whining, or I'll send for the typhoons!"

Earth also screamed: "If you don't stop I'll run the rivers dry and make the land quake!"

Tao only got angrier and angrier. He knew he was wrong, but he was really furious. And the work was so very boring! He screamed back at Earth: "I don't care if you run the rivers dry, and quake all you want. Hah!" Then, turning to Sky, he pointed an angry finger and said: "And as for you—bah! Send all the typhoons you want if that will make you happy." And he pounded all the harder.

Sky and Earth tried very hard to keep their tempers. After all, Tao was their dear friend even if he was foolish and insolent sometimes. At last Sky spoke softly: "The trouble with you is that you're too impatient. Just look how you're ruining the rice by pounding it so hard."

But Tao only stamped his feet on the ground. Then he raised the pestle again and began to pound the rice still harder. "Thud! thud! thud!" He pounded so that when he raised the pestle it hit Sky, and when he brought it down into the mortar, the blow jarred Earth.

"Hey! stop it!" cried Sky. "You're pushing me up with that pestle."

"Hey! stop it!" cried Earth. "You're pushing me down with that pestle."

Tao pounded harder and faster. He shouted back: "And if you don't stop scolding me, I'll keep right on pushing up and beating down —pushing up and beating down!" And the pestle and mortar kept going "Thud! thud! thud!"

The harder Tao pounded the angrier he became. Then, after a final mighty "Thud!" he rushed into his hut and grabbed Moon and Star Belt from their places.

Rushing back outside, Tao threw Moon at Sun where it hung in

51

Sky's hair and hit Sun straight in the face. Then he threw Star Belt at Sky with such force that the belt broke and the thousands of stars were scattered over Sky's hair.

How confused everything was! The three quarreling friends screamed and shouted and cried. Day and night came and went in only a few seconds as Sun and Moon glinted and glowed together. The stars blinked and twinkled, dancing about aimlessly.

Sky and Earth were enraged. "Now see what you've done!" they screamed at Tao.

Gradually Tao's anger turned to fear. He was beginning to feel sorry for what he had done. But he was too proud to say so. Instead he began pounding the rice again—"Thud! thud! thud!"

Up and down went the pestle—"Thud! thud! thud!"—and with

each stroke Sky was pushed farther up and Earth was pushed farther down. "Thud! thud! thud!"—and up went Sky, with Sun and Moon and Stars in its hair. "Thud! thud! thud!"—and down went Earth, carrying Tao with it.

And presently the sky had risen so high that even a thousand men standing on each other's shoulders could not have reached it. And the earth had fallen so low, carrying the man with it, that Tao's voice could never reach the sky again.

Tao was tired, so very tired, and he felt very, very sorry for what he had done. He was sorrier still to have lost his good friends. Sky was lost to him forever. Earth stayed with him out of pity, but it never spoke to Tao again.

As for his treasures, Tao never got back his two lamps and his belt of stars; they stayed in the sky, where they gradually found their right places so that nights and days followed one after another again. Tao could see his lost treasures shining in the sky, the sun during the day and the moon and the thousands of stars during the night. All that was left to him was his guitar and his mortar and pestle. Sometimes you can still hear him strumming the guitar and singing. Sometimes you can still hear his pestle going "Thud! thud! thud!"

Retold by Elizabeth M. Gonzales
Illustrated by Emerson Cunanan

53

Mr. Ripe and Mr. Raw

Once upon a time there was a husband and wife who had two daughters. Like all parents, they loved their children dearly. And like all Thai parents in the old days, they felt their most important duty was to find good husbands for their daughters.

The girls' names were Im and Oon. Im was the older, and one day the father began talking to his wife about her. "Im is very good at cooking and sewing and gardening," he said, "and it's time that she married. We must find a very smart man for her husband."

"All men are stupid," said his wife. "If you wait until you find a smart husband for her, she'll die an old maid."

"No, you're wrong. There's Mr. Ripe, who has already asked me if he can marry Im. He already calls me Father. I'll tell him tomorrow that he can marry her."

"Is that what you call a smart man? He may seem smart to you, but—"

"He certainly is smart! Why, he's already taken orders." (In those days, a young man of Thailand usually spent some time as a lay monk in a Buddhist temple.) "He told me himself that he became a monk several years ago. Ah, Mr. Ripe!—he'll make the best son-in-law we could possibly have. He's the husband for our Im. He's the smartest man in the whole country."

"Well, if that's that, I have something to say too. As for Oon, I don't care whether her husband has taken orders or not, just so long as I like him. And I like Mr. Raw. He's the husband for Oon."

"What! He hasn't even become a monk. And he's as green and stupid as his name. Mr. Raw indeed! No, I won't allow Oon to marry him."

"All right! If you won't allow Oon to marry Mr. Raw, I won't allow Im to marry Mr. Ripe. So there!"

This settled the matter, and soon Im married Mr. Ripe and Oon married Mr. Raw. The two young men came to live in the home of their wives' parents. The father-in-law still couldn't stand Mr. Raw and was always finding fault with him, but he was the mother-in-law's favorite and she always took his side.

One day the father-in-law wanted to go to a rice field that was quite far away. He had his wife prepare lunches and then he and the two young men set out by boat. Mr. Ripe rowed in front, Mr. Raw rowed in back, and the honorable father-in-law sat in the middle.

On the way they saw some pelicans happily floating on the water and playing together. The father-in-law said: "Why are pelicans able to float, Ripe? Come, tell your father why."

"Because they have such thick feathers, Father," answered Mr. Ripe.

Pleased with this answer, the father-in-law turned to Mr. Raw and said: "And what do you say, ha?"

Mr. Raw answered: "Why, it's only natural for them to float."

Before long they heard some storks crying loudly to each other. The father-in-law said: "Why do storks cry so loudly, Ripe? Come, tell your father why."

"Because they have such long necks, Father," answered Mr. Ripe.

Pleased with this answer, the father-in-law yelled at Mr. Raw: "And what do you say, ha?"

Mr. Raw answered: "Why, it's only natural for them to cry loudly."

They rowed on. Presently they saw, on a nearby bank, a clump of bamboo with red leaves outside and green leaves inside. Pointing to the bamboo, the father-in-law said: "Why are the leaves green inside and red outside, Ripe? Come, tell your father why."

"Because the red leaves outside are in the sun and the green leaves inside are in the shade, Father," said Mr. Ripe.

Pleased, the man yelled at Mr. Raw: "And what do you say, ha?"

Mr. Raw answered: "Why, it's only natural."

As they rowed on, they came to two rice fields. One was bare, with no plants and no trees, while the other was filled with all kinds of vegetation. The father-in-law asked Mr. Ripe why the two fields were so different. Mr. Ripe answered that the barren field had some salt water from the sea running through it, while the fertile field had only fresh water. Again the father-in-law asked Mr. Raw and again came the same answer: "It's only natural."

As soon as they returned home from their trip, the man began to scold

57

his wife in a loud, angry voice, blaming her for having chosen such a stupid son-in-law as Mr. Raw.

Later, when they were eating supper, the wife said to her favorite son-in-law: "Tell me, Raw, what did you do to make Father so angry?"

So Mr. Raw told what had happened: "Father asked why pelicans can float, and Brother Ripe said it was because they have such thick feathers. But I said it was only natural for them to float. Well, now, a coconut doesn't have feathers, but it too can float, can't it?

"Then Father asked why storks can cry so loudly, and Brother Ripe said it was because they have such long necks. But I said it was only natural. Well, now, frogs and toads don't have long necks, but they too can cry loudly, can't they?

"Then Father asked about the bamboo leaves, and Brother Ripe said the outside leaves were red because they were in the sun and the inside leaves were green because they were in the shade. But I said it was only natural. Well, now, what about watermelons? Isn't their green *outside* in the sunlight and the red *inside* where the sun never reaches?

"Then Father saw two rice fields, one barren and the other fertile, and Brother Ripe said they were different because one had salt water in it and the other had fresh water. But I said it was only natural. Well, now, what about a baldheaded man? Does the sea water run through his head? And yet he too is bald, isn't he?"

From that day onward the father-in-law never made fun of Mr. Raw again. In fact, he now liked him as much as he liked Mr. Ripe. Apparently he had come to realize that, just as it is with all men, for his sons-in-law to be whatever they were, stupid or smart, was only natural.

Retold by Sunit Prabhasawat
Illustrated by Manat na Chiang Mai